THIS BLOOMSBURY BOOK

BELONGS TO

....

THIS BOOK BELONGS TO

. . . .

This is where we start—at my own ~~book~~ story at the top of the bookcase. we've covered up the old boring title with the new one. And here's

→ THE NEW CONTENTS ←

1. THE BEGINNING — jolly exciting!
2. THE MIDDLE — thrilling!
3. THE END — fairy tale (I hope!)

So at the ~~bigining~~ start of my old story, it's actually the start of a super new one — it's time that books had their own ~~adventures~~! I can hear the bookroom clock chiming ~~for~~ the hour to begin now (watch for the clocks on every page counting the hour down!) — Hey ho! I hear a plaintive cry for HELP, so now at last (Can't wait!) it's time for..... →

BLOOMSBURY
CHILDREN'S
BOOKS

First published in
Great Britain in 2000 by
Bloomsbury Publishing Plc
38 Soho Square,
London, W1D 3HB

This paperback edition first published 2001
Text and illustrations copyright © Jonny Boatfield 2000
The moral right of the author / illustrator has been asserted

A CIP catalogue record of this book is available from the British Library
ISBN 0 7475 5083 2 (Paperback)
ISBN 0 7475 4470 0 (Hardback)

Printed in Hong Kong by South China Printing Co.

1 3 5 7 9 10 8 6 4 2

— Introductions —

Twilight, Two-lights, the magic hour between day and night, when the Bookpeople can come to life!

When the clock chimes the hour, Twilight begins. The Cruel Ape Kidnaps the Little Girl, and Little Tom, with his faithful mutt Trash, must give chase, but they have to rescue her before the hour is up, or they will be 'Clocked'— stuck outside their books for anyone to find!

Outside, the birds are falling silent, the world is becoming still, whilst here inside, the magic is about to begin....

...So now there's just time to meet some of the characters who will share this great adventure with you......

LITTLE TOM + TRASH

Hello everyone!

Wuff!

CLAGGY

SOPPY KIDS BOOK!

SOPPY RABBITS.

FINE FINE

THE CRUEL APE

Hur Hur...

FIND ALL 21 OF HIS BANANA SKINS.

THE LITTLE GIRL

FOLLOW HER TRAIL OF PAGES.

So, Outside, on the Twilit bookshelf......

......and far down below, on the Bookroom carpet.......

ANOTHER DAY IN THE

On Planet Waterless, the Fish can Fly

There's something wrong with this picture. Can you tell what it is? Answer on p.7

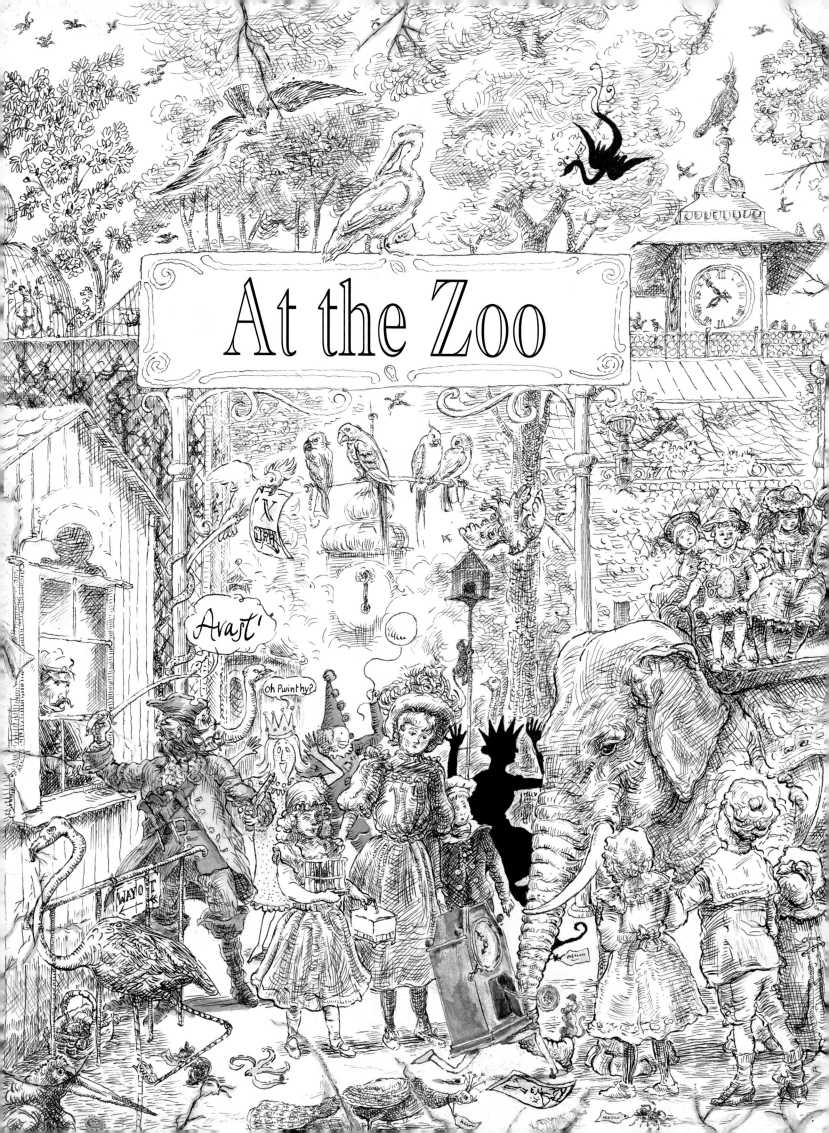

Acclaim for *The Twilight Book*

'Half-book, half-game – his [Jonny's] eccentric line drawings fizz with activity and charm ... enough to keep the reader poring over this book well after lights-out' *The Times*

Enjoy more great picture books from Bloomsbury ...

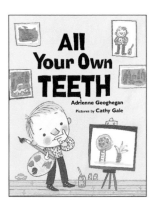

Beetle Boy
Lawrence David &
Delphine Durand

Be Good, Gordon
Angela McAllister &
Tim Archbold

All Your Own Teeth
Adrienne Geoghegan &
Cathy Gale

Wizzil
William Steig &
Quentin Blake